Sam Walter Foss

Songs of War and Peace

Sam Walter Foss

Songs of War and Peace

ISBN/EAN: 9783337181642

Printed in Europe, USA, Canada, Australia, Japan

Cover: Foto ©Andreas Hilbeck / pixelio.de

More available books at **www.hansebooks.com**

Songs of War and Peace

BY

SAM WALTER FOSS

AUTHOR OF " BACK COUNTRY POEMS," "WHIFFS FROM WILD MEADOWS,"
" DREAMS IN HOMESPUN," ETC.

———

BOSTON
LEE AND SHEPARD PUBLISHERS
10 MILK STREET
1899

Who will write the best song, who will paint the best picture,
    Whose music is best?
He who understands man, knows the heart of him, loves him
    Above all the rest.

Put stars in your song and put skies in your picture,
    Put mountains and seas;
But one heart-throb that's tuned to the heart of a brother
    Is greater than these.

Man first in your song; man first, and then mountains,
    And the woods and the seas;
And know, while you picture the star groups of midnight,
    He is greater than these.

What is art, what is art and the artist's achievement,
    Its purpose and plan?
'Tis the message that's sent from the heart of the artist
    To the heart of a man.

iv

CONTENTS

Contents

SONGS OF WAR AND PEACE

WAR

I am War. The upturned eyeballs of piled dead
    men greet my eye,
And the sons of mothers perish — and I laugh to
    see them die —
Mine the demon lust for torture, mine the devil lust
    for pain,
And there is to me no beauty like the pale brows of
    the slain!
But my voice calls forth the godlike from the slug-
    gish souls at ease,
And the hands that toyed with ledgers scatter thun-
    ders round the seas;
And the lolling idler, wakening, measures up to
    God's own plan,
And the puling trifler greatens to the stature of a
    man.

When I speak the centuried towers of old cities melt
    in smoke,
And the fortressed ports sink reeling at my far-
    aimed thunder stroke;
And an immemorial empire flings its last flag to the
    breeze,
Sinking with its splintered navies down in the un-
    pitying seas.
But the blind of sight awaken to an unimagined day,
And the mean of soul grow conscious there is great-
    ness in their clay;
Where my bugle voice goes pealing slaves grow he-
    roes at its breath,
And the trembling coward rushes to the welcome
    arms of death.

Pagan, heathen, and inhuman, devilish as the heart
    of hell,
Wild as chaos, strong for ruin, clothed in hate un-
    speakable —
So they call me — and I care not — still I work my
    waste afar,
Heeding not your weeping mothers and your widows
    — I am War!
But your soft-boned men grow heroes when my flam-
    ing eyes they see,
And I teach your little peoples how supremely great
    they be;

Yea, I tell them of the wideness of the soul's un-
folded plan,
And the godlike stuff that's moulded in the making
of a man.

Ah, the godlike stuff that's moulded in the making
of a man!
It has stood my iron testing since this strong old
world began.
Tell me not that men are weaklings, halting trem-
blers, pale and slow —
There is stuff to shame the seraphs in the race of
men — *I know.*
I have tested them by fire, and I know that man is
great,
And the soul of man is stronger than is either death
or fate;
And where'er my bugle calls them, under any sun
or star,
They will leap with smiling faces to the fire test of
war.

THE DIALOGUE OF THE SPIRITS

———

Says the Spirit of To-day to the Spirit of All Time,
   " Have you seen my big machines?
My fire steeds, thunder-shuttlecocks that dart from
     clime to clime,
Hear the lyrics of their driving rods, the modern
     chant sublime — "
Says the Spirit of To-day to the Spirit of All Time,
   " Have you seen my big machines? "

" Hear the thunder of my mills," says the Spirit of
     To-day,
   " Hear my harnessed rivers pant.
Men are jockeys with the lightnings, and they drive
     them where they may,
They are bridlers of the cataracts that dare not say
     them nay,
And the rivers are their drudges," says the Spirit of
     To-day.
   " Hear my harnessed rivers pant."

Says the Spirit of All Time to the Spirit of To-day,
   " Haste and let your work go on.

Tap the fires of the underworld to bake your bread,
　　I say;
Belt the tides to sew your garments, hitch the suns
　　to draw your sleigh."
Says the Spirit of All Time to the Spirit of To-
　　day,
　　" Haste and let your work go on."

" But," says the Spirit of All Time to the Spirit of
　　To-day,
　　" Tell us, how about your men?
Shall they, like live automatons, still drudge their
　　lives away,
When the rivers, tides, and lightnings join to help
　　them on their way? "
Says the Spirit of All Time to the Spirit of To-
　　day,
　　" Tell us, how about your men?

" Yes, harness every river above the cataract's brink,
　　And then unharness man.
To earth's reservoirs of fire let your giant shaftings
　　sink,
And scourge your drudging thunderbolts — but give
　　man time to think;
Throw your bridles on the rivers, curb them at the
　　cataract's brink —
　　And then unharness man."

Says the Spirit of All Time: " In this climax of the
    years
  Make no machine of man.
Your harnessed rivers panting are as lyrics in my
    ears,
And your jockeyed lightnings clattering are as mu-
    sic of the spheres,
But 'tis well that you remember, in this climax of
    the years:
  Make no machine of man."

SAM PASCO AND NAPOLEON

NAPOLEON took Europe and tossed down toppling
    thrones,
And strewed its ghastly hillsides with white and
    bleaching bones ;
And dandled kings like puppets and made his world-
    uproar,
And played his battailous music, passed, and was
    heard no more.

Sam Pasco took a run-down farm, a run-down farm,
    alas !
Where stretched unbroken solitudes between each
    spear of grass.
And moss usurped its hillsides and flags usurped
    its meads,
And both its hills and meadows were a tragedy of
    weeds.

Sam Pasco's hard campaigning ! Long waged the
    stubborn fray ;
And Sam grew bowed and battered, and Sam grew
    seamed and gray ;

But those bald hills grew green with grass, and ap-
    ple-blossoms fair
Stormed, as with storms of winter, the fragrant
    summer air.

Napoleon took Europe and played his mighty game,
And sowed its fields with corpses and wrapped its
    towns in flame.
Sam Pasco took his run-down farm and greened
    its moss-gray soil,
And one small plat of this wide earth was fairer
    through his toil.

Sam Pasco and Napoleon! Wide are the midnight
    skies,
And in the wideness of the worlds men seem of
    equal size ;
And from some star may each look down, each
    stretch his phantom arm,
Napoleon tow'rd Austerlitz, Sam Pasco tow'rd his
    farm.

THE WORLD-SMITHS

———

WHAT is this iron music
   Whose strains are borne afar?
The hammers of the world-smiths
   Are beating out a star.
They build our old world over,
   Anew its mould is wrought,
They shape the plastic planet
   To models of their thought.
This is the iron music
   Whose strains are borne afar;
The hammers of the world-smiths
   Are beating out a star.

We hear the whirling sawmill
   Within the forest deep;
The wilderness is clipped like wool,
   The hills are sheared like sheep.
Down through the fetid fenways
   We hear the road machine;
The tangled swamps are tonsured,
   The marshes combed and clean.

We see the sprouting cities
  Loom o'er the prairie's rim,
And through the inland hilltops
  The ocean navies swim.

Across the trellised land-ways
  The lifted steamers slide;
Dry shod beneath the rivers
  The iron stallions glide;
Beneath the tunnelled city
  The lightning chariots flock,
And back and forth their freight of men
  Shoot like a shuttlecock.
The moon-led tides are driven back,
  Their waves no more are free,
And islands rise from out the main
  And cities from the sea.

We see the mountain river
  From out its channel torn
And wedded to the desert
  That Plenty may be born;
We see the iron roadway
  Replace the teamer's rut;
We see the painted village
  Grow round the woodman's hut.
Beneath the baffled oceans
  The lightning couriers flee;

Across the sundering isthmuses
   Is mingled sea with sea.

Smiths of the star unfinished,
   This is the work for you,
To hammer down the uneven world —
   And there is much to do.
Scoop down that beetling mountain,
   And raze that bulging cape;
The world is on your anvil,
   Now smite it into shape.
What is this iron music,
   Whose strains are borne afar?
The hammers of the world-smiths
   Are beating out a star.

THE SHADIGANDIAN REFORMER

I'M a moral regulator, and I feel it is my mission
To keep my fellow-citizens from travelling to perdi-
tion ;
I feel my mission in my bones, I'm made to regulate
The morals of my fellow-men and keep my neigh-
bors straight.

I hunt for sin on every trail, through wood and
swamp and mire,
And when I drive it from its lair I lift my gun and
fire ;
I hunt the sin through hidden ways, through many
a covert path,
And pulverize the sinner with the thunder of my
wrath.

Born was I in a sinful age, a sinful neighborhood ;
My fellow-townsmen all were bad, and not a soul
was good.
So, in this town of Shadigand, when I was young
and strong,
I told the Shadigandians that they were foul with
wrong.

My neighbors' sins filled me with grief almost beyond
    control.
The weight of Shadigandian sin was heavy on my
    soul.
" I 'll make this place as virtuous as any in the land,
I'll make," said I, "a virtuous town this town of
    Shadigand.

" The time will come," I said, " twill come when sin
    will disappear,
When in this town will not be found a single sinner
    here."
And I have done the thing I said — a work of some
    renown —
For now, to-day, there is not left one sinner in the
    town.

I'd meet men on the highways and I'd show them
    they were bad,
And give them all a catalogue of all the sins they had;
I'd greet them in the fields at work and look them
    in the eye,
And cry aloud and spare them not and smite them
    hip and thigh.

I'd follow them to market, and I'd follow them to
    mill,
And show their gross perversities of thought and
    deed and will;

And then I'd seek them in their homes, and preach
    for days and days,
And show to them the fearful wrong and error of
    their ways.

And I convicted them of sin ; they all began to go ;
Yes, they all trickled out of town in one continuous
    flow ;
And my own wife and family departed with the rest,
And left this town of Shadigand an unpolluted nest.

And so my prophecy came true that sin would dis-
    appear —
There's not one sinner left in town — I'm all the
    soul that's here.
But you, sir, you're a sinful man — foul sin your
    soul has hid —
What's that ? You're going to leave the town ?
    Just what the others did.

OUR LITTLE BACK STAR

Oh, we do fairly well on this little back star,
   This world in the suburbs of space,
Though we're out here alone, and we hardly know
      how
   To get our belongings in place.
We've no other models to which to conform,
   We've no other star for a plan,
And we think for a young and a little back star,
   We have done nigh as well as we can.
And so we abide here with things as they are
In our cosmical suburb, our little back star.

'Tis mostly unfinished, our little back star,
   (Takes time for a world to get made),
And the building of worlds is involved in delay
   Not known to the carpenter's trade.
" 'Tis not the best possible star?"   No, not yet;
   Takes time to build worlds, I repeat.
And the long, long design of its architect's plan
   Is a few billion years from complete.
And we hardly can guess what the finished worlds are
In the unfinished state of our little back star.

There are noisy complaints of our little back star,
  There are voices upraised that are loud ;
And there's much that is said that is nigh to the
    truth
  By the lips of the querulous crowd.
There is much that is lacking in justice and truth,
  There is more that is lacking in grace;
So our little back star with its querulous freight
  Whirls on through the suburbs of space.
And the great frontward stars from their stations
    afar,
In silence look down on our little back star.

Oh, the great frontward stars may be eons ahead
  Of our little back star in the race,
But the simple, sole thing for a star and a man,
  Is to look their own fate in the face.
There's a long race ahead for our little back star,
  And failures and flouts not a few,
But perhaps in a score of a thousand of years
  We may grow up a Shakespeare or two.
We are bound on a journey that stretches afar,
There's a long course ahead for our little back star.

Our little back star rolled on with its freight,
  In the crude early years of its prime,
With wallowing monsters that sprawled in the sun,
  And dragons that weltered in slime.

Let the voices upraised that are loud in complaint
　　Still swell from the querulous crew ;
But our little back star travels on knowing well
　　What a few million ages can do.
So some in wise silence are gazing afar
Down the long distant path of our little back star.

PIONEERING

I

SONGS for the tameless tamers,
  The tamers of the seas;
Songs for the stout old sailors
  Who harnessed every breeze,
Who through the seas of darkness
  By unknown winds were whirled;
Proud Drake and stout Magellan,
  The girdlers of the world.

And songs for Henry Hudson,
  Wherever he may be,
Whose bones have bleached three hundred
    years
  Beneath his northern sea.
Songs for the grim old sailors,
  Men of heroic pith,
Yea, songs for old John Cabot,
  And songs for brave John Smith.

Songs for La Salle, the dauntless,
  And songs for strong Champlain;

For good Marquette and Joliet,
   For Crockett, Boone, and Kane.
Songs for the pioneer vanguard,
   Who ploughed uncharted floods,
And laid the sites of cities
   Within the roadless woods.

II

Songs for all pioneering,
   And all are pioneers:
All sailors from an anchorage
   That fronts the tide of years.
And each man sails an ocean
   No other sailed before,
And each man findeth for himself
   An undiscovered shore.

Sail on across the morning,
   Sail forth beyond the night,
Sail forth and trust the eternal winds
   To blow your bark aright;
And every day shall greet you,
   New phase of wave or breeze,
The moonlight on new headlands,
   The sunlight on new seas.

Still sail the tameless tamers,
   The tamers of the seas;

Still sail the stout old sailors
   Who harness every breeze;
Still through the seas of darkness
   By unknown winds are whirled
Proud Drakes and stout Magellans,
   The girdlers of the world.

SWIPESEY, THE MISSIONARY

CHRIS'MUS is comin'! Let 'er come!
  I've jined the Mission Band
What sends out clo'es an' grub an' things
  To ev'ry heathen land.
I loves them little heathen kids
  So sunk in sin an' wrong,
An' I have jined the Mission Band
  To help them kids along.
Ya-as, I have jined the Mission Band,
  It's jest the thing for me,—
For all who jine, nex' Chris'mus time,
  Will git a present.   See?

Them heathen kids is low-down mugs,
  They lies an' swears an' fights,
An' crawls into a hole, like bears,
  To go to bed at nights.
I wants to help them kids along,
  To better livin' win 'em.
An' I'm perpared to smash the bloke
  That says a thing ag'in 'em.
I love them heathen kids, I does,
  I've jined the Mission Band,

An' I will git a present. Gee!
  Nex' Chris'mus. Understand?

Them heathen kids is wickud things,
  An' growin' wuss an' wuss.
I wants to make 'em noble. See?
  An' sweet an' good, like us.
I wants to make the gang bang-up,
  Jest like us kids is here,
An' elervate the hull blame crowd
  'Way up to our idear;
An' so I've jined the Mission Band,
  Me an' me brudder John,
We'll git a present Chris'mus time —
  You tumble? Are ye on?

I loves them little heathen kids,
  An' though they're mighty tough,
We're goin' to elervate the scamps,
  An' this 'ere ain't no bluff.
We means to make them heathen kids
  As good as Buck Magee,
As Swipesey Dugan, Slugger Sam,
  Or Guff Malone or me.
An' so we've jined the Mission Band,
  Me an' me brudder John,
We'll git a present, Chris'mus time —
  You tumble? Are ye on?

THE COMING CAPTAINS

THERE are many children dressed in bibs,
There are many sleeping in their cribs,
There are many playing with their toys,
There are many girls and many boys:
They're coming! Though the world is wide,
Make room! They're coming! Stand aside!

Is there a wrong that needs a blow
From sturdy arms to lay it low?
Are there, albeit the world is old,
Unconquered evils manifold?
Has wrong some fortress wall unscaled?
Some bastioned tower unassailed?
Some vaunting champion undefied?
Stand back! They're coming! Stand aside!

And are there dragons still unslain,
The wallowing monsters of disdain,
Who mock the voices of our time
With reptile hisses from their slime?
And do the hearts of strong men fail
When they behold their serpent trail?

The boys and girls are coming.   Stay!
The dragons they have had their day.

Are there old phantoms of old fears
That haunt the pathway of the years?
Old doubts that make the sunshine cold
And make the hearts of men grow old?
Fall back! ye spectres, in the night,
Our face is forward toward the light.
The boys and girls are coming!   Hide!
Stand back!   They're coming!   Stand aside!

The old commanders have grown gray,
The famous Captains pass away,
The grim old Generals are slain —
Now who shall plan the new campaign?
There are many children dressed in bibs,
There are many sleeping in their cribs —
Come forward!   Our old chiefs are gone!
Come from your cradles — lead us on!

The army murmurs at delay;
Come, lead us, Captains.   We obey.
Hark, hear the loud foes' battle-drum,
Ye captains from the cradle, come!
The hosts meet.   Let the war begin !
We love you — trust you — you will win.
Haul down, ye foes, your flag of pride !
Fall back !   They're coming !   Stand aside !

THE WIDE-SWUNG GATES

———

THE Genius of the West
    Upon her high-seen throne,
Who greets the incoming guest
    And loves him as her own ;
The Genius of these States
    She hears these modern pleas
For the closing of the gates
    Of the highways of her seas.
"Fence not my realm," she says, " build me no
    continent pen,
Still let my gates swing wide for all the sons of
    men."

The Genius of these States,
    She of the open hand,
Stands by the open gates
    That look to every land :
"Come hence " (she hears the groans,
    The distance-muffled din
Of millions crushed by thrones),
    "Come hence and enter in.

Shut not my gates," she says, "that front the in-
    flowing tide,
For all the sons of men still let my gates swing
    wide."

    "What! leave thy bolts withdrawn?"
      Cry they of little faith,
    "For Europe's voided spawn,
      Spores of the Old World's death?
    These monsters wallowing wide
      In anarchy's black fen?"
    "Peace, peace, it is my pride
      To make these monsters men;
With the Great Builder work that knows not Greek
    or Jew,
And from an old-world stuff fashion a world anew.

    "And in my new-built state
      The tribes of men shall fuse,
    And men no longer prate
      Of Gentiles and of Jews:
    Here seek no racial caste,
      No social cleavage seek,
    Here one, while time shall last,
      Barbarian and Greek:
And here shall spring at length, in narrowing caste's
    despite,
That last growth of the world, the first Cosmopolite.

"A man not made of mud
    My coming man shall be,
But of the mingled blood
    Of every tribe is he.
The vigor of the Dane,
    The deftness of the Celt,
The Latin suppleness of brain
    In him shall fuse and melt;
The muscularity of soul of the strong West be blent
With the wise dreaminess that broods above the
    Orient.

"Here clashing creeds upraise
    Their warring standards long,
Till the ferment of our days
    Shall make our new wine strong.
Let thought meet thought in fight,
    Let systems clash and clinch, —
The false must sink in night,
    The truth yields not an inch.
No thought left loose, ungyved, can long a menace
    be
Within a tolerant land where every thought is free."

The Genius of the West
    Upon her high-seen throne
Thus greets the incoming guest
    And clasps him as her own.

The Genius of these States
　　Puts by these modern pleas
For the closing of the gates
　　Of the highways of her seas.
"Fence not my realm," she says, "build me no
　　continent pen,
Still let my gates swing wide for all the sons of
　　men."

THE SONG OF THE CANNON

WHEN the diplomats cease from their capers,
  Their red-tape requests and replies,
Their shuttlecock battle of papers,
  Their saccharine parley of lies;
When the plenipotentiary wrangle
  Is tied in a chaos of knots,
And becomes an unwindable tangle
  Of verbals unmarried to thoughts;
When they've anguished and argued profoundly,
  Asserted, assumed, and averred,
Then I end up the dialogue roundly
  With my monosyllabical word.

Not mine is a speech academic,
  No lexicon lingo is mine,
And in politic parley, polemic,
  I was never created to shine.
But I speak with some show of decision,
  And I never attempt to be bland,
I hurl my one word with precision,
  My hearers — they all understand.

It requires no labored translation,
    Its pith and its import to glean ;
They gather its signification,
    They know at the first what I mean.

The codes of the learnèd legations,
    Of form and of rule and decree,
The etiquette books of the nations—
    They were never intended for me.
When your case is talked into confusion,
    Then hush you, my diplomat friend,
Give me just a word in conclusion,
    I'll bring the dispute to an end.
Ye diplomats. cease to aspire
    A case that's appealed to debate,
It has gone to a court that is higher,
    And I'm the Attorney for Fate.

A RECIPE FOR SUCCESS

———

How is it I have prospered so?   How is it I have
    struck
Throughout the hull of my ka-reer jest one long
    streak of luck?
Intellijunce, young man; that's all.   I reason an'
    reflec' —
'Tis jest intellijunce an' brains an' straightout in-
    tellec'.

W'en I git up I'm allus sure to dress me right foot
    first,
Or put my drawers on wrong side out, or hev my
    vest reversed,
For them are signs you'll hev good luck; an eddi-
    cated man
Knows all them signs, an' shapes his life on a con-
    sistent plan.

I've strewed ol' hoss-shoes down the road for some-
    thin' like a mile,
An' I go out an' hunt 'em up a-every little while;

For if you fin' a hoss-shoe, w'y, you're sure to pros-
    per then;
A fac' that is familyer to all eddicated men.

A cat's tail p'intin' to'rds the fire, it is an awful
    sign;
But I hev counteracted it with every cat of mine;
If my cat's tail should p'int that way it wouldn' give
    me scares;
I'd go in my back entry then an' simply fall up-stairs.

It's a good sign to fall up-stairs an' counteracts the
    cat;
An' that's the way I shape my life, I balance this
    with that.
I see four crows — bad sign I know — might scare
    a man that's bolder;
But I jest wait an' see the moon rise over my right
    shoulder.

The moon it counteracts the crows; one balances
    the other,
For one is jest wiped out, you see, an' cancelled off
    by t'other.
I hear a dog howl in the night; it don't give me no
    dread,
I balance it by gittin' out the right han' side the
    bed.

An' so I've prospered all my life by jest a little
    pains.
Intellijunce, young man, that's all, an' intellec' an'
    brains.
'Tis ignorunce that makes men fail. An' wisdom —
    nothin' less —
Inlightenmunt an' knowledge, sir, can bring a man
    success.

THE SONG OF A RIVER

I

Hear my song of a river,
Its calm and its strife ;
'Tis the song of a river,
The song of a life.

AFAR amid benignant hills in caverns of deep shade,
'Neath rippling arches of cool leaves, within a for-
    est glade,
The mountain rivulet leaps down in silvery cascade.
Child of the hills, it sings its song and spills its
    wayward glee
In tangled music through the rocks and dreams not
    of the sea,
It spills ambrosial morning joy and dreams not of
    the sea.

And there are many-colored birds that join their
    mingled strain,
And many zephyr-tumbled leaves that swell the
    strong refrain,
And the voice of the sombre pine alone is the only
    voice of pain.

'Tis the only voice that tells of the sea that's
    under sun or star,
And a foolish, phantom voice to the stream that
    dreams the sea is far,
That dreams that the world is a mighty world and
    the sea is very far.

But birds from the south fly into the hills and sing
    of a world unknown,
And there are winds that float from the west from
    odorous valleys blown,
And the winds that tell of a meadowy land with
    deep grass overgrown ;
And a land beyond the meadowy land at the end of
    a winding glen,
A steaming land and a strenuous land, the Land of
    the Roar of Men —
And the river is fain for the meadowy land and the
    Land of the Roar of Men.

II

Hear my song of a river,
Its calm and its strife ;
'Tis the song of a river,
The song of a life.

And the river leaps to the meadowy land and is
    strong in the stress of its flow,

It is hurled by the weight of its floods above and is
   mad for the deep below,
For it hastens on to the falls ahead where the mead-
   owless cities grow.
And it leaps the falls and joins in the noise of the
   Land of the Roar of Men,
Till it yearns for the peace of the sleeping hills
   and the deeps of the woodland glen —
By the giant wheels of the thunderous mills it
   yearns for the woodland glen.

And the spindles clash in the thunderous mills and
   the work of the world is done,
And men are hived from the breath of the hills and
   the glory of the sun,
And the lives of men are ravelled out, but webs of
   cloth are spun.
Through its darkened sluice of builded stone its
   writhing waters flee,
Till it yearns for the meads of the salted tide and
   the voice of the calling sea,
For the tolerant plains of the tided meads and the
   voice of the friendly sea.

And it flows to the meads of the salted tide and is
   cheered by the ocean's roar, ·
For in the roar is a mystic Voice that speaks forevermore,

A mystic Voice in a mystic song that sings of a
thitherward shore.
And the river is calm with the calm of the Voice
and through the salted lea,
In the silent trance of a pleasant sleep it falls in
the waiting sea —
Falls lulled by the croon of the mystic song in the
mother arms of the sea.

> *My song of a river,*
>   *Its calm and its strife ;*
> *My song of a river,*
>   *The river of life.*

A BROOK AND A LIFE

I

I KNOW a brook that flits and flows
  Where many a water-lily grows;
That leaps with singing down the hills,
  Then sleeps in meadows of repose.
I know a brook whose silvery sheen
Gleams through its arbored banks of green,
Then dashes down a mad ravine, —
    I know a brook:
    But till its latest mile is gone
    A brook must ever travel on.

This brook I know is fed by rills
That tumble from the singing hills,
This brook leaps down its bowldered banks
  And far its liquid music spills.
Then flows where deep-toned pines complain,
And whippoorwills pour their song of pain
To the unpitying night in vain —
    This brook I know:
    For till its latest mile is gone
    A brook must ever travel on.

And then it sweeps from out the gloom
To turn the mill and whirl the loom,
And draws a nurture from the night
That makes its water-lilies bloom.
It has its days of gloom and glee,
Its dark pine woods and lighted lea, —
And then 'tis lost within the sea,
    This brook of mine:
  For till its latest mile is gone
  A brook must ever travel on.

II

I know a life that flits and flows
Where many a water-lily grows,
That dances down the singing hills,
And sleeps in meadows of repose.
I know a life, that, like a stream,
Has caught the glory and the gleam
Of many a white cloud's floating dream.
    I know a life:
  And till its latest hour is gone
  A life must ever travel on.

I know a life whose winding ways
Have flowed through leagues of sunny days,
And gathered music for its song
From meadow larks and woodland lays.

This life I know has flowed alone
Where groves of pine make solemn moan,
Has flowed by night when no star shone —
      This life I know:
    For till its latest hour is gone
    A life must ever travel on.

    And then it leaped from out the gloom
    To turn the mill and whirl the loom,
And drew a nurture from the night
      That made its water-lilies bloom ;
Though swollen by the rain of tears,
Or smiled on by the sunny years,
The sea's far voice is in thine ears,
        O life I know !
    And till thy latest hour is gone
    Toward that dim sea flow bravely on.

THE BROOK AND THE BOY

I

" Oh, the hills are fair where I shall flow,"
    Said the song of the brook to the boy;
" And the meadows are sweet to which I go,"
    Said the song of the brook to the boy;
" For I flow on to a broader land,
    To scenes where wider vales expand,
    To a land where lordlier mountains stand,"
    Said the song of the brook to the boy."

" And I go into a broader land,"
    Said the heart of the boy to the brook;
" To the towered towns and the cities grand,"
    Said the heart of the boy to the brook.
" Oh, the coming day draws near, and then
    I will leave this dreary woodland glen —
    A leader of men in a world of men,"
    Said the heart of the boy to the brook.

II

" Ah, me, for the peace of the hills again,"
    Said the song of the stream to the man, —

"The brooding peace of the woodland glen,"
  Said the song of the stream to the man.
"And, oh, for the rest of the quiet glade,
  And the dreaming peace of the alder shade,
  And the vales where the smiles of the morning
     played,"
  Said the song of the stream to the man.

"And, oh, for the meadows of youth once more!"
  Said the heart of the man to the stream;
"And the dewy hope of the days of yore!"
  Said the heart of the man to the stream.
"And, oh, for the strength of its sunrise joy,
  When living was play and the world was a toy;
  And, oh, for the hope of the heart of a boy!"
  Said the heart of the man to the stream.

FARRAGUT TO DEWEY

SAID the Goddess of Fame to the pedestalled
    shade
  Of Farragut looming on high:
" Move over a bit on your pedestal, man,
  For a twin-born of Fame draweth nigh;
Move over a bit, give him room at your side,
  A trifle of space you must spare
For the first of the sons of the sea of our day,
  So make room for Dewey up there."

"And who is this Dewey?" the gray shade replies.
  "He is one of your sailors," said Fame;
"And the sea-winds that blow on both sides of
    the world
  Are loud with the sound of his name.
Without losing a ship, or a gun, or a man,
  Spain's navy he sunk in the sea."
Said Farragut then to the new son of Fame:
  "Approach, and come up here with me!"

TWO BRIDES

I

THE Man who Loved the Names of Things
    Went forth beneath the skies,
And named all things that he beheld,
    And people called him wise.
An unseen presence walked with him
    Forever by his side,
The wedded mistress of his soul, —
    For Knowledge was his bride ;
She named the flowers, the weeds, the trees,
And all the growths of all the seas.

She told him all the rocks by name,
  . The winds and whence they blew;
She told him how the seas were formed,
    And how the mountains grew;
She numbered all the stars for him
    And all the rounded skies
Were mapped and charted for the gaze
    Of his devouring eyes.
Thus, taught by her, he taught the crowd ;
They praised — and he was very proud.

II

The Man who Loved the Soul of Things
   Went forth serene and glad,
And mused upon the mighty world,
   And people called him mad.
An unseen presence walked with him
   Forever by his side,
The wedded mistress of his soul, —
   For Wisdom was his bride.
She showed him all this mighty frame,
And bade him feel — but named no name.

She stood with him upon the hills
   Ringed by the azure sky,
And shamed his lowly thought with stars,
   And bade it climb as high.
And all the birds he could not name,
   The nameless stars that roll,
The unnamed blossoms at his feet,
   Talked with him soul to soul;
He heard the Nameless Glory speak
In silence — and was very meek.

SURVIVALS

I

A THOUSAND acorns through the mould,
One summer in the days of old,
  Burst forth into the sun and breeze
  To grow into a thousand trees,
To fight the storm and brave the cold,
  And live through many centuries.

There came a keen, untimely frost;
Five hundred infant oaks were lost.
  And then the herds that chanced that
    way,
  The browsing kine and lambs at play
Among the hillocks greenly mossed,
  Cropped down four hundred in a day.

A hundred oaks were left to grow,
But fourscore perished in the snow ;
And of the score that still remain
  Ten fall before the hurricane,
Ten challenge all the winds that blow
  And cast their shade o'er all the plain.

But, as the years pass on, one oak
Lies shattered by the thunder-stroke,
 And one is felled, the woodman's prey ;
 One falls through it's own heart's decay ;
One in the whirlwind's fury broke,
 And two the torrents swept away.

Four oaks now toward the sun aspire ;
One falls before an earthquake dire,
 And one is dragged away in chains
 A keel to plough the ocean plains ;
One withers in a forest fire,
 And one — one only oak — remains.

And there it stands, the centuries' pride,
The monarch of the mountain side,
 Blessed by five hundred summers bland,
 By breaths of ferny fragrance fanned ;
But no one notes the oaks that died —
 They are forgotten in the land.

II

Each summer 'mid the waste and weeds
Doth Nature sow immortal seeds,
 And scatter over field and fen,
 Through tumbled gorge and babbling
  glen,
The seeds of men of mighty deeds,
 Seeds of a thousand deathless men.

A thousand men of loftier strain,
Of ampler soul and subtler brain,
     By Nature's unexhausted hand
     Are sown each year in every land —
Strong men, and dowered to attain
     The heights where the immortals stand.

But many in a sordid age
Yield up their birthright heritage,
     And, scorched by traffic's poison breath,
     Their germ of grandeur withereth ;
For tinsel. tags, and equipage
     They give their better parts to death.

And some forget their mighty trust
Through weakness mixed with human dust ;
     They burn with phosphorescent fire
     Engendered in the slime and mire ;
Are torn by tigers of their lust,
     And slain by dragons of desire.

And some from their high path depart
Through inborn cowardice of heart ;
     Some fall unnoted in the stress
     Of their unneighbored loneliness ;
Some freely choose the baser part,
     And greatness yields to littleness.

And some whose tainted blood is rife
With poison at the core of life,

Who cry, " The fault is not in us ! "
But Fate will pause not to discuss —
They perish in the unequal strife
    Who fight with beasts at Ephesus.

And some send out their branching shoots,
But perish from unwatered roots ;
    Some, smit by sorrow's thunder-stone,
    Go down at midnight and alone ;
Some, charmed by pleasure's shawms and
      flutes,
    Play no high music of their own.

III

A thousand men were sown broadcast —
Mayhap but one survives at last.
    He shapes our thoughts and rules our
      ways,
    And lives an endless length of days,
And mates the mighty of the past,
    Enshrined in Pantheon pomp of praise.

Immortal are the songs he sings,
And deathless is the word he brings ;
    Aye, deathless is his very breath,
    Far, far his long thought journeyeth ;
But, ah ! his termless life — it springs
    From the dark soil of many deaths.

THE AWAKENING OF UNCLE SAM

"Oh, Uncle Sam," they said, "has grown fat and
    loves his ease,
And he lingers long at table and distends his grow-
    ing girth;
The strong arm we used to know has grown slug-
    gard-like and slow,
And they mock his smug indifference to the ends
    of all the earth.

"As his money bags grow heavy does his love of
    man grow small,
As his cushioned chair grows softer does his cal-
    loused heart grow hard;
He is careless of his fame and the glory of his
    name,
And the vision of the prophet and the rapture of
    the bard.

"And the tyrants in their anger lash their slaves
    before his eyes,
And he turns his sleepy features tow'rd their faces
    hot with tears,

And he sits between his seas in his soft, voluptuous
    ease,
And the voices of their torment smite his undis-
    cerning ears."

Ah, the slander of the tongues that proclaimed his
    heart was cold !
Ah, the error of the dotage that believed his arm
    was weak !
Ah, the folly, mad and dire, that provoked the slow
    to ire,
And the pride that's in the careless, and the might
    that's in the meek !

He has risen from his feasting, the old look is on
    his face,
For the voices of the helpless and the dying throng
    his path,
For he sees at last their tears, and their groans are
    in his ears,
And his arm is clothed with thunder, and his heart
    is nerved with wrath !

We have wronged him, the forbearing, him the
    patient, slow to smite,
And we love him more than ever and are prouder
    of his fame;

And we weep the taunts we uttered and the whispered sneers we muttered —
For his guns before Manila silenced all the tongues
   of blame.

PETER, THE ORTHODOX

———

"PETE, you're a common laughing-stock,
  You are the village butt,
 Your hair is so outrageous long —
  Why don't you get it cut ?"
"Bekase dere ain't no barber, sah,
  Dat's good ernuff foh me;
 Dere ain't no barber in dis town
  Dat's up to my idee."

"Why, there is 'Rastus Graham, Pete,
  A barber up to par."
"La! yes; but den I kain't hev him,
  Foh he's a Baptis', sah.
 No low-down Baptis' herertic
  So bigotty ez he
 Shall never cut de ha'r upon
  A Meferdis like me."

"But Pratt's a barber just as good
  As any on the list;
 A splendid barber, and besides
  An earnest Methodist."

"He am a Meferdis, I know,
    But I kain't train wiv Pratt
Bekase I am a 'Publican
    An' he's a Dimmerkrat."

"But there is Bangs, a Methodist,
    A very righteous man,
A Methodist in high repute,
    A good Republican."
"But he's a homerpaff, the wretch,
    Ez bad ez he can be,
An' he kain't cut de wool on sich
    An allopaff ez me.

I stan's foh righteousness, I does,
    Foh troof an' nuffin' less;
No Baptis' trash an' homerpaffs
    Can suit my piousness.
W'en some good barber comes to town,
    A Meferdis fair an' squar',
An allopaff an' 'Publican,
    W'y, he can cut my ha'r."

THE WORDLESS VOICE

A DWELLER in a hut alone, fed from a dish of wood,
A drinker of the flowing brook, a child of solitude,
A sleeper on a bed of leaves, may find that life is
    good,
And hear high music on his way that bids his soul
    rejoice,
If his wise ear has learned to hear — to hear the
    Wordless Voice.

The Wordless Voice it speaks not in the syllables
    of men;
'Tis borne along the night wind down the glimmer-
    ing of the glen;
It talks among the rushes in the fluttering of the fen ;
It flows along all valleys where any brook can flow,
Where any stream can catch the gleam of sunlight
    or of snow.

It speaks beside all pathways that wind beneath all
    trees,
And speaks from all the chanting shores that circle
    all the seas,

And from the hills that know no plough, and from
    the spadeless leas,
It speaks a language, not of men, but plainly un-
    derstood,
By men who love, below, above, all things and
    deem them good.

The noises blown about the world beneath the scorn-
    ful stars,
The cannons of the Captains and the thunder of the
    wars;
The sound that tears the jangled years and all their
    music mars,
Cannot drown down the Wordless Voice that from
    the silence speaks;
'Tis blown to men from every glen and floats from
    all the peaks.

Dark for the world would be the day that saw that
    Voice withdrawn;
Then would the day be emptiness, the race of men
    but spawn;
No twilight peace would fall at night, no hope would
    come with dawn;
No dreams would haunt the sky line, no fancies
    throng the glen;
The wretched weight of iron fate would crush the
    hearts of men.

Up from the deeps of silence the awful mountains
rise,

And in the deeps of silence are arched the sacred
skies,

And in the peace of silence sleep the eternities;

And from the soul of silence that was ere time
began

Comes forth the Voice that bids rejoice and speaks
its word to man.

THE YEAST OF EVOLUTION

THE yeast of evolution was dropped into the welter
Of the drifting sea of chaos long ago;
And then the cloud-shapes gathered and the world-
     stuff floated mistlike,
   Till the pulp of stars was hardened and the worlds
     began to grow.

And the yeast of evolution worked upon the plastic
     planets,
   And our fire-world bubbled mountains to the sky;
And our continents emerging shook the sea from off
     their highlands,
   And the red-jawed dragons wallowed where all life
     but theirs would die.

And the yeast of evolution worked into the blood of
     dragons,
   And they perished and their bellowing died away;
And the slowly mellowing cycles rolled their slow-
     paced revolutions,
   And the primal Man came forward and stood
     naked to the day.

And the yeast of evolution grew within his aimless
    purpose,
  And the hairy savage battled, clan with clan,
Till the strong-armed brute grew conscious of a
    deeper life within him,
  And the soul of man grew conscious and revealed
    itself to man.

Then the yeast of evolution works its great amelio-
    ration,
  And the World Tree sheds its blossoms through
    the gloom,
Till it flowers into Moses, Homer, Plato, Dante,
    Shakespeare, —
  Flowers prophecies of flowers that are yet to
    burst in bloom.

For the yeast of evolution works, as hitherto, for-
    ever;
  We are in the morning hours of our day;
Down the ever-widening vista whose long stretches
    end in twilight
  We shall come on new perfections, meet new
    music on the way.

Yea, the yeast of evolution works, as hitherto, for-
    ever;
  Far are now the wallowing dragons in their slime;

Ah, but farther, farther, farther, is the long, long way
　　before us,
　We shall meet a loftier music down the thorough-
　　fare of time.

THE PULLING-THROUGH OF TODLUM

———

THE crossest man in Glosterkonk,
Without no doubt, is Dr. Bronk.
Ol' Dr. Bronk hez got a jaw
That's firmer than the morril law,
An' Dr. Bronk hez got a frown
That purty nearly knocks ye down.
Gee! he is sot an' stiff an' tough,
An' made of linkum vity stuff.
W'en He comes in a sick room he
Kicks up etarnal bobbery;
He jaws because the air's too het,
An' 'cause he finds the winders shet;
He's jest ez like to scold ez not
'Cause the cold water is too hot;
An' then, nex' minute, he will scold
'Cause the hot water is too cold.
He scares the women from their wits,
An' gives the nurse conniption fits;
An' w'en he's there they want to die,
An' w'en he's gone they set an' cry.
But we love Dr. Bronk, we do;
For Dr. Bronk pulled Todlum through.

But there are few in Glosterkonk
Who waste much love on Dr. Bronk,
For even gentle Elder Priest
Says he is savage as a beast;
An' Abram Murch an' Hiram Howe
Say they wouldn' hev him to a cow;
An' that good soul, A'nt Hester Pratt,
Sez she wouldn' hev him to a cat,
Wouldn' hev the pesky critter nigh
Onless she wished the cat to die.
" Ol' vinegar is honeycomb
Compared to him," said Deacon Home.
" A bear's a gentleman," said Jim,
" A gentleman compared to him."
Wall, maybe all these things are true,
But Bronk, he pulled our Todlum through.

Young Todlum he was very sick,
An' we got smilin' Dr. Dick;
He tol' us 'twas no use to try;
A hopeless case; the child mus' die.
"Git Dr. Brown!" my wife she cried.
He came; the child had almost died.
"No use," said Dr. Brown. "Too late!
No use, good friends, to fight with fate."
An' then my wife she turned to me,
" Run quick an' git ol' Bronk!" said she.
An' ol' Bronk came. How he did swear

About the closeness of the air;
Threw off three quilts upon the floor,
An' bellered out, " Don't shet that door ! "
He sent us flyin' here an' there,
An' everything we did he'd swear.
He kept us in a tremblin' plight,
For everything we did warn't right.
But we held in — didn' make a sound —
An' let the ol' bear thunder 'round.
He kept us jumpin' all night long,
An' everything we did was wrong.

At daylight Todlum gave a groan,
A still, faint, awful kind o' moan !
" He's going ! He's going ! " my wife she cried,
An' fell down sobbin' at his side.
" Don't bawl so, woman ; can't yer see
Yer cub is goin' to live," sez he.
Todlum looked up, the blessed child !
Into his mother's face an' smiled.
" Don't make sich thunderin' hullabaloo,"
Said Bronk, " I've pulled the rascal through."

" Don't make such thunderin' hullabaloo ;
Get up ! I've pulled yer rascal through."
The sweetest words that ever rung
From any seraph angel's tongue
Were not so sweet as these he said

While we were standin' roun' that bed.
My wife she threw her arms around
That ol' bear's neck with one glad bound ;
Her face was in his whiskers hid,
She hugged an' kissed him — yes, she did !
The sweetest words we ever heard,
Although, I guess it soun's absurd,
Were just them words that ol' Bronk said
While we were standin' roun' that bed :
"Don't make sich thunderin' hullabaloo,
Get up ! I've pulled yer rascal through."

THE DOME OF PICTURES

In a little house keep I pictures suspended; it is not a fixed house,
It is round, it is only a few inches from one side to the other;
Yet behold, it has room for all the shows of the world, all memories!
Here the tableaux of life and here the groupings of death.

WALT WHITMAN.

AH, each man bears his Dome of Dreams —
    A picture dome
Whereon are painted homely cares,
Defeats and triumphs and despairs;
    A gallery thronged with wider themes
        Than those of Rome.

    The pictures on this Dome of Dreams
        Are memories.
Young Barefoot wandering through the dew,
Through daisied fields when life was new,
    By woodland paths, by lilied streams
        And blossomed trees.

    The picture of a maid at school
        With floating hair:
Transfigured in the mist is she
On that dim shore of memory,
    Life's dewiness about her, cool
        And pure and fair.

The picture of a road that leads
        From an old home :
A boy that from a wooded swell
Looks through his tears and waves farewell —
    Then down through unknown hills and meads
        Afar to roam.

The pictures of the long, long way
        He travelled far;
Fair fruited hillsides slanting south,
Baked herbless uplands smit with drouth,
    And night paths with no gleam of day —
        Without a star.

And pictures of wide-sleeping vales
        And storm-tossed waves;
Of valleys bathed in noonday peace,
Of sheltered harbors of release ;
    And glimpses of receding sails;
        Of open graves.

And pictures of fair islands set
        In golden foam ;
And pictures of black wrecks upcast
On barren crags by many a blast —
    But on !   Life paints more pictures yet
        Upon that dome.

WHEN HE HAS AN IDEA IN HIS HEAD

No mountains can stand in the way of a man
   Who has an idea in his head,
No whirlwinds can blow him away from his plan
   When he has an idea in his head.
He is scared by no menace of mountainous seas
Or the heavens sowing thunderbolts wide on the
     breeze —
If his idea is large, it is larger than these —
   When he has an idea in his head.

The loud sons of thunder may bellow their wrath
   When he has an idea in his head,
The tumult of tongues welter over his path
   When he has an idea in his head ;
The sound of the shouters may sound in his ear,
The blare of the babblers environ him near —
He stalks through their jangle with never a fear,
   When he has an idea in his head.

He has looked in the face of the famine and smiled
   When he had an idea in his head,
Bared his neck to the axe with a soul reconciled
   When he had an idea in his head;

He has stood in the flame with a light in his eye
That outshone the fire that blazoned the sky;
They burned him to cinders — his thought did not
    die,
    When he had an idea in his head.

Shall we padlock his lips?   Shall we handcuff his
    hands
    When he has an idea in his head?
Shall we fetter his feet and his arms with steel
    bands
    When he has an idea in his head?
Very well; we will bind him, a feasible plan,
Let us bind him and all of his pestilent clan —
But where is the halter can tie such a man
    When he has an idea in his head?

No, no; turn him loose; turn him loose among men
    When he has an idea in his head;
Let him carry his message to city and glen
    When he has an idea in his head.
Yes, hold back the tides from the shore, if you can,
And hold back the bolt from the cloud with your
    ban —
But woe to the man who would fetter the man
    Who has an idea in his head.

UNCANONIZED SAINTS

NOT all the saints are canonized :
  There's lots of 'em close by;
There's some of 'em in my own ward,
  Some in my family;
They're thick here in my neighborhood,
  They throng here in my street ;
My sidewalk has been badly worn
  By their promiscuous feet.

Not all the heroes of the world
  Are apotheosized ;
Their names make our directories
  Of very ample size ;
And almost every family
  Whose number is complete,
Has one or more about the board
  When they sit down to eat.

Not all the martyrs of the world
  Are in the Martyrology ;
Not all their tribe became extinct
  In some remote chronology.

Three live ones talked with me to-day,
　　Five passed me with a bow,
I met a dozen at the store, —
　　There goes a couple now !

The ichthyosaurus is extinct,
　　The great auk is no more ;
But heroes, martyrs, saints, are thick
　　As in the days of yore.
Not like the auk and mastodon
　　Whose bones alone are found,
These are the types that still persist
　　And evermore abound.

Why weep for saints long dead and gone ?
　　There's plenty still to meet ;
Put on your wraps and call upon
　　The saints upon your street.
Oh, Plutarch's heroes were strong souls
　　And men of parts and pith, —
But there's McPeters and O'Brien,
　　Stubbs, Anderson, and Smith.

And Foxe's martyrs were strong souls,
　　But still their likes remain :
There's good old Mother Haggerty,
　　And there is sweet Aunt Jane.

You know them just as well as I,
    Since they're a numerous brood,
For they are with you all, and live
    In every neighborhood.

THE HIGHER CARELESSNESS

I

It happened in the days of old
Brahm gave a man an egg to hold.
" Hold ye this egg," he said, "and learn
To bide in peace till I return."
Then from the earth a mist upreared
Wherein the great Brahm disappeared.

II

The self-same hour in days of old
Brahm gave a man a rod to hold,
And said, "This rod is grooved to gears
Whereby I guide the moving spheres;
This is the lever rod whereby
I move the worlds that throng the sky.
Hold ye this rod," he said, "and learn
To bide in peace till I return."
Then through a thunder-cloud he steered,
And mid the lightnings disappeared.

III

The man who held the egg turned pale,
And his weak heart began to fail.
"Ah," groaned he, " by what vain decree
Did Brahm assign this egg to me?
This universe is ruled, 'tis plain,
By fickle gods of little brain;
The worlds roll on in aimless dance
To jangled tunes of brainless chance;
Men are but animated clods,
The trifling playthings of the gods;
The universe is built on guess,
Its base is laid on nothingness;
And Brahm, he plays a monster's part,
And deep I hate him from my heart."
His heart grew cold in awful doubt,
His hand relaxed — the egg dropped out,
Fell to the earth without delay,
And smashed, as eggs will smash to-day.

IV

The man who held the awful rod
Mused on the greatness of the god,
Upon the wisdom of his plan;
The awful majesty of man;
The great eonian goals whereto
The worlds are moved the ages through;

The cycles of the cosmic range,
Their upward sweep from change to change;
The soul of goodness at the core
Of nature's heart forevermore;
And all his soul was ravished by
The spheral music harmony.
"Brahm plays," he said, "a father's part,
And deep I love him from my heart."
So, rapt in wonderment sublime,
He lost the sense of space and time,
And musing on the ways of God —
Forgot his charge and dropped the rod.

V

Then through the deeps of space were hurled
The wrecks of many a shattered world;
And many a sun in aimless flight
Shot flaming through chaotic night;
From their eternal stations high
The stars forsook the reeling sky;
And Chaos oped its Stygian deep,
(Drowsed in eternities of sleep),
To crown Creation's final curse,
And gulp the ruined universe.

VI

Then Brahm returned, and waved his hand
In silent gesture of command,

And moved tow'rd Chaos' seething swim,
And called the wild suns back to him.
And, back from bournless gulfs of space,
Each star returned to his own place.
And then, with a benignant nod,
He called the man who dropped the rod.
The man who dropped the egg drew near,
And stood before the god in fear.

VII

Then to the man who dropped the rod
He said, " Thou art beloved of God;
And unto thee henceforth is given
The guidance of the lower heaven."
But said to him who dropped the egg:
" I see that thou art still a dreg;
I re-incarnate thee anew
Into a worm —for 'tis thy due.
Be beast, bird, reptile of the fen
Ere thou emerge a man agen.
A thousand cycles must be run
Ere thou, as man, shalt see the sun."
" I only dropped an egg," said he,
" Then why impose this curse on me?
And why not give to him thy curse —
This man who dropped a universe?
But unto him a place is given,
Vicegerent of the lower heaven."

" Ah, learn," said Brahm, " the eternal fact,
It is the thought behind the act,
And not the act, I bless or ban,—
The motive, not the deed, of man.
He loved, while thou didst hate. Depart —
Depart, and be the worm thou art."

JUPITER PLUVIUS, JR.

I STAND, in evening's shade withdrawn,
  Mid twilight's dusky forms,
A Jupiter Pluvius of the lawn,
  A local god of storms.
Not mine Jove's thunderbolts which clove
  The blasted heath and holt;
I hold the storms of Pluvian Jove
  Without his thunderbolt.
The nozzle of my hose I press,
  And proudly take my stand;
I stand and pour my thunderless
  Tornadoes on the land.

I grasp the nozzle of my hose,
  And proudly I opine
Old Adam's Eden life was prose
  Compared to life like mine.
Why for his hoseless garden sigh,
  And for his hoseless day?
For what's a garden when it's dry
  Without a hose, I say?
And so with joy I walk about,
  And thread the evening gloom,

And lug my wandering waterspout
    And portable simoom.

The little toads look up to me,
    And though they all are dumb,
They think : " Our mighty deity,
    The god of storms, has come.
From his benignant hand doth fly
    The rain he giveth free,
He holds the cisterns of the sky,
    The fountains of the sea ;
His gracious storms new hopes infuse
    Through all the fainting land —
Behold the mighty oceans ooze
    Forever from his hand."

Outside my yard the hot dog star
    Rules with malefic sway —
My hose turns back the calendar,
    Within my yard, to May ;
I heed not August's fiery thrill,
    For well I understand
A man can carry, if he will,
    His climate in his hand.
Then turn the nozzle of your hose
    In any clime or zone,
And make, the while its current flows,
    A climate of your own.

The hand that may not hold the sword,
  Or guide the ship of state,
Or write the poet's burning word,
  Or do the deeds of fate;
The feeble hand of little worth
  For battle or for blows
May add new freshness to the earth
  By turning on the hose.
The nozzle of my hose I press,
  And proudly take my stand;
I stand and pour my thunderless
  Tornadoes on the land.

MOTHER ASIA

Mother Asia, we stand at your threshold.
  In a far immemorial yore
We left you, great Mother of Nations,
  And now we return to your door.
We have circled the seas and their islands,
  We have found us new worlds in the main,
We have found us young brides o'er the alien
    tides —
  Now we come to our mother again.

We wandered through ages unnumbered,
  We were mad with the fever to roam,
But the new flag that waves at Manila
  Proclaims that your sons have come home.
There are weeds in the Gardens of Morning,
  There are mildew and dearth and decay,
And your blind days are drear and your heart
    has grown sere
  The years that your sons were away.

But turn your old eyes to the seaward
  Where the flag of the West is discerned.

Be glad, gray old Mother of Nations,
　The youth of the world has returned.
They come with the wealth of their wanderings,
　They come with the strength of their pride ;
Now, old mother, arise and lift up your dim
　　eyes —
　Behold your strong sons at your side !

They will toil in your Gardens of Morning,
　They will cleanse you of mire and fen ;
You shall hear the glad laughter of children,
　You shall see the strong arms of young men.
New hope shall come back to your borders,
　Despair from your threshold be spurned,
A new day shall rise in your Orient skies —
　The youth of the world has returned.

GRASSVALE'S GREAT MAN

You wouldn't suppose a man like me, a hayseed sort
    er chap,
Who hain't no special intellec' nor brains beneath
    his cap;
You wouldn't suppose I'd hev a son who'd be a
    genyus, hey?
A man who'd climb the height er fame and then
    set down an' stay.

I've allus been a plain ol' duff, an' Bill he was my
    son;
I s'posed he'd do the kind of work thet I hed allus
    done;
Chop cord-wood, dig pertaters, hoe corn, an hol' the
    plough,
An' settle down an' chew his cud contented as a
    cow.

But Bill he warn't that kind er stuff, for, born for
    mighty things,
He vowed that he'd hol' up his head with intellec-
    chul kings;

An' now he's gone an' done it; he's a man of great
  renown,
An' Grassvale now has give the worl' a great man
  from the town.

He's gone off to the city; everybody knows him
  there,
An' he stan's there for ten hours a day, right in the
  public square:
An' he's a big policeman there, an' stan's there in
  the street,
An' straightens out the tangle w'en the teams an'
  street-cars meet.

An' everybody's scat of him. He jest hol's up his
  hand,
An' the hummin' slam-bang 'lectric car will come
  right to a stand;
The cars an' teams an' kerridges an' hacks will all
  stan' still, —
For ev'ry blessed soul of 'em is scat to death of Bill.

An' he's the boss of all the street, he stan's there
  in the swim,
An' no one dares to move until they git permish of him.
He waves his hand — the teams go on — he lifts it,
  an' they stop —
To think a humble boy like Bill should climb so near
  the top.

An' this ere is my son, my boy.   I never dreamed I'd
  be
The father of a genyus so tremendous high as he ;
But in this lan' the poorest lad may make himself
  a name,
An' a poor humble kid, like Bill, may climb the
  heights er fame.

MY PROPERTIES

I own no park, I keep no horse,
    I can't afford a stable,
I have no cellar stored with wine,
    I set a frugal table ;
But still some property is mine,
    Enough to suit my notion :
I own a mountain toward the west,
    And toward the east an ocean.
Just this one mountain and one sea
Are property enough for me.

A man of moderate circumstance,
    A frugal man, like me,
With one good mountain has enough,
    Enough with one good sea.
My mountain stretches high enough,
    Up where the clouds are curled ;
My ocean puts its arms around
    The bottom of the world.
I do not fear my sea will dry ;
My hill will last as long as I.

I cannot glibly talk with men,
    No gift of tongues have I ;
My sea and mountain talk to me,
    Expecting no reply.
They tell me tales I may not tell,
    But tales of cosmic worth,
Of conclaves of the early gods
    Who ruled the infant earth ;
Tales of an unremembered prime
Told by Eternity to Time.

And so I'm glad the mountain's mine,
    I'm glad I own the sea,
That they have special privacies
    Which they impart to me.
It took eternity to learn
    The tales they know so well,
And I am glad these tales will take
    Eternity to tell.
I do not fear my sea will dry;
My hill will last as long as I.

UNCLE SAM'S SPRING CLEANING

———

"THERE has been a heap of rubbish dumped about
    the patient seas,
And all cleaning hitherto has been a sham;
It is time for my spring cleaning — and I hope you
    catch my meaning —
For I'm going to clean 'em out," says Uncle Sam.
    "And I'm going to rinse 'em down,
    And I'm going to soak 'em out,
And I'm going to sponge 'em off and make 'em clean;
    And I'll do a handsome job with my scrubbing
    brush and swab,
And I'll give a different aspect to the scene.

On the Philippines, a dumpground for the mediæval
    truck
And the old miasmal rubbish heaps of Spain,
I began my vernal cleaning — and I think they
    know my meaning —
For I turned my hose upon them at full strain.
    And I guess I swabbed 'em down,
    And I guess I rubbed it in,
And I guess I swashed 'em off and made 'em clean;

And when I've wiped 'em dry with my army mop,
      says I,
There'll be a different aspect to the scene.

And I'll clean off Porto Rico and I'm going to wipe
      it dry,
   And poor filth-infested Cuba must be clean ;
Four hundred years of lumber that its rubbish holes
      encumber —
   If you wait you'll see it burn like kerosene.
            And I guess I'll soap 'em down,
            And I guess I'll scour 'em off,
And I guess I'll turn my hose on at full strain ;
   And then, when I am through, then old Cuba will
      be new,
And there won't be any rubbish heaps of Spain.

She has blotted all the oceans and I'll wipe her off
      the seas,
   And I'll cleanse the cluttered islands of her slime ;
And this is just the meaning of my vigorous spring
      cleaning —
   Fate's washing-day has come — and it is time
            And I guess when I have soaped 'em,
            And I guess when I have wrung 'em,
And I guess when I have hung 'em out to dry,
   Not a single blot of Spain on an island shall remain,
And I think that they'll feel cleaner then, says I."

THE ONLY MAN IN THE WORLD

I LIVED in a hut on a mountain high,
   On its bowldered summit curled;
A snow-storm fell on the mount, and I
   Was the only man in the world.

The snow and the sky and the stars in their course
   Were all that I could see;
And I was alone with the Universe,
   And the Universe with me.

Around my hut the winds were whirled,
   And the stars looked down to see;
As I was the only man in the world,
   They told their tales to me.

The heart of the world to the heart of a man,
   When the world and the man are alone,
Tells tales that few since the world began
   Have ever heard or known.

And often I sigh, where the crowds sweep by
   And the human tides are whirled,
For the hut on the pathless mount where I
   Was the only man in the world.

r

THE RUSE OF JOHN P. JOCK

YES, I'm the Shagbark County Bard. An' so you
    come to see
How I attained my wide renown an' popularity?
I ain't no flower to blush unseen, an' I don't crawl,
    yer see,
A poor unreco'nized galoot to all eternity.

The *Shagbark County Clarion* wouldn't take a word
    I wrote,
Its editor's a ignorant, uneducated goat;
If I'd been a common genius, I'd a languished on
    unknown —
But I ain't no wilted violet to droop beneath a
    stone.

So I got a man to write to him, " If he would kindly
    print
That most transcendent piece of verse known as
    ' The Demon's Hint.' "
So I got a man to send it in — I had it in my frock —
" I send ' The Demon's Hint,' " he wrote, " by Mr.
    John P. Jock."

The editor he printed it, the author's name and all.
Next week an old subscriber asked for " Lines on
    Early Fall."
Another fellow sent them in, an' wrote, " I've al-
    ways held
These lines on ' Fall ' by John P. Jock are surely
    unexcelled."

Next week a fellow asked him for " The Mystery of
    the Stars,"
A piece "that had consoled his life through many
    jolts an' jars."
I got a man to send it in — as reg'lar as a clock —
Who wrote, " I send these wondrous words by Mr.
    John P. Jock."

Next day he got a postal card that gave his soul a
    shock,
"Cut down your editorials and publish more of Jock."
" Give us more Jock," the words came up from all
    parts of the State,
"More poetry by John P. Jock, a man supremely great."

So I'm the Shagbark County Bard; an' now, my
    friend, you see
How I attained my wide renown an' popularity.
I ain't no flower to blush unseen, an' I don't crawl,
    yer see,
A poor unreco'nized galoot to all eternity.

THE FRIENDLY, FLOWING SAVAGE

The friendly and flowing savage, who is he?
WALT WHITMAN.

THE friendly, flowing savage, this is his proof and
test:
 He is low as the lowest
 And high as the highest
 And good as the best.
And he goes forth and learns of men.
 The whole world is his school,
 The bad man and the good man,
 The learned man and the fool.
 The proud man and the meek man,
 The great man and the small;
The friendly, flowing savage absorbs and loves them
all.

The friendly, flowing savage, he eats the meat of
life,
 Loves the stress of its battle,
 The rush of its onset,
  The pride of its strife.

His hand is facile to the axe,
    And supple to the pen,
And the jack-plane and the crowbar —
    He is a man of men.
The desk man, school man, field man,
    Of coarse or finer clay,
The friendly, flowing savage is coarse and fine as
    they.

The friendly, flowing savage, he has wise ears to
        hear ;
            The sounds of the sidewalk,
            The clink of the kitchen,
                Are sweet to his ear.
He loves the rhythm of the axe,
    The schooner's flapping sheet ;
And the babe's cluck and the boy's shout
    And the girl's laugh, all are sweet.
And the slave's groan and the child's sob,
    And the great cries and the small ;
The friendly, flowing savage, he hears and feels
        them all.

The friendly, flowing savage, his heart is wise to
        feel
            The joy of the victors,
            The shame of the conquered,
                Their woe and their weal.

It vibrates to the playground's shout,
　　And the sound of swords that smite
When the hate of years and the pride of kings
　　Come to the clash of fight.
And the world's shouts and the world's groans,
　　Its heart throbs, great and small;
The friendly, flowing savage, he knows and feels
　　them all.

THE PAGEANT

THE hand of time is free and unconfined,
  And sows its wide delights;
It sows the lavish days among mankind,
  And sows the sumptuous nights.
It sends the June-tide's pulsing overflow
Crested with foam of roses all ablow,
And flaunts the flying banners of the snow
  From all the wintry heights!

Bosomed in beauty of the night and day,
  The glories of the year,
Man gropes amid the grandeur on his way
  To grasp inglorious gear.
Ah, could he see the splendors round him throng,
The Pageant of the Vision sweep along,
Then every soul would be a priest of song
  And every man a seer.

The pageant of the vision still sweeps on,
  The ages come and flee;
The beauty of the long years that have gone
  Forevermore shall be.

And age by age the eyes of men shall gaze
On beauty, clearer with the fleeing days,
Till every voice shall raise the hymn of praise —
　For every eye shall see.

THE TREE LOVER

WHO loves a tree he loves the life that springs in
    star and clod;
He loves the love that gilds the clouds and greens
    the April sod;
He loves the Wide Beneficence. His soul takes
    hold on God.

A tree is one of nature's words, a word of peace to
    man,
A word that tells of central strength from whence
    all things began,
A word to preach tranquillity to all our restless clan.

Ah, bare must be the shadeless ways, and bleak the
    path must be,
Of him who, having open eyes, has never learned to
    see,
And so has never learned to love the beauty of a
    tree.

'Tis well for man to mix with men, to drive his
    stubborn quest

In harbored cities where the ships come from the
    East and West,
To fare forth where the tumult roars, and scorn the
    name of rest.

'Tis well the current of his life should toward the
    deeps be whirled,
And feel the clash of alien waves along its channel
    swirled,
And the conflux of the eddies of the mighty-flowing
    world.

But he is wise who, 'mid what noise his winding
    way may be,
Still keeps a heart that holds a nook of calm
    serenity,
And an inviolate virgin soul that still can love a
    tree.

Who loves a tree he loves the life that springs in
    star and clod,
He loves the love that gilds the clouds and greens
    the April sod;
He loves the Wide Beneficence. His soul takes
    hold on God.

WHEN PETER SANG

WHEN Peter sang the rafters rang,
　He made the great church reel;
His voice it rang a clarion clang,
　Or like a cannon's peal.
Yes, Peter made the rafters ring,
　And never curbed his tongue;
Albeit Peter could not sing,
　Yet Peter always sung.
Ah, wide did he his wild voice fling
　Promiscuous and free;
Despite the fact he could not sing,
　Why, all the more sang he.
　　With clamorous clang
　　And resonant bang
　His thunders round he flung;
　　He could not sing
　　One single thing:
　Yet Peter always sung.

The choir sang loud, and all the crowd
　Took up the holy strain;

But Peter's bawl rose over all
  Tempestuously plain.
The organ roared, and madly poured
  Its music flood around,
But Peter drowned its anthem loud
  In cataracts of sound.
The people hushed, the choir grew still,
  Still grew the organ's tone,
Then Peter's voice rose loud and shrill,
  For Peter sang alone.
      His clamorous shout
      Had drowned them out,
  And silenced every tongue ;
      He could not sing
      One single thing:
  Yet Peter always sung.

When Peter died the people cried,
  For Peter he was good,
Although his voice produced a noise
  Not easily withstood.
Though many cried when Peter died
  And gained his golden lyre,
They nursed a heartfelt sympathy
  For heaven's augmented choir.
They knew where'er his soul might be
  Loud would his accents ring.

He'd sing through all eternity
    The songs he could not sing.
      The heavenly choir
      He'd make perspire
  And heavenly arches ring;
      Though he can't sing
      One single thing,
  For evermore he'll sing.

A THINKER ON THINKERS

OUR good ol' Elder Hombleton he said he thought
     I ought
To git acquainted with the lords an' emperors of
     thought;
He said I had sich nateral capacities of mind
That I ought to git familiar with the thinkers of
     mankind.
An' so he fetched me Shakespeare's plays, an' Mil-
     ton's poems, too,
An' ol' George Eliot's novels next for me to waller
     through.
An' so I wallered through 'em all, read through the
     whole long shelf:
An' all the more I read their stuff the more I loved
     myself.

W'y, now, jest look at Shakespeare: poof! that
     foolish people praise.
He made a terrible mistake to go to writin' plays,
The man couldn't think; he rambles on and jumps
     from this to that,
An' I dunno, an' he dunno, jest w'at he's drivin' at.

I've thought more thoughts, out here to work ; I've
    thought more in one day,
More genyuine thoughts than he could stick in one
    whole ramblin' play.
There might be good plays written, sir ; plays
    number one an' prime —
But I must carry on my farm, an' I hain't got the time.

Now there's John Milton's poetry that makes sich
    hullaballoo,
'Tain't sense, 'tain't rhyme, 'tain't argiment, an' I
    don't b'lieve it's true.
They call him a great thinker, hey ? His thoughts
    are great an' high ?
If he's a thinker, Lord alive ! Good Gracious !
    w'at am I ?
He's got some gift for words, I know ; but he can't
    string 'em. See ?
Can't string 'em so they'll make a thought that
    holds up an idee.
There might be poetry written, sir, chockfull of
    thought sublime.
But I must carry on my farm, an' I hain't got the time.

Now, there's George Eliot's novels, wall, I never
    seen the man,
An' I wouldn't hurt his feelin's, but the stuff he
    writ, I swan !

He tries to tell us stories, but he hain't got none to
  tell;
W'y, I could tell 'em twice as quick, an' forty times
  as well.
But I've jest wallered through 'em all, read through
  the whole long shelf,
An' all the more I've read the stuff the more I've
  loved myself.
But there might be novels written that would be
  first-class and prime;
But I mus' carry on my farm, an' I hain't got the
  time.

THE SONG OF THE HOE

HEAR ye the song of the hoe,
  And hear ye without scorn;
The ring of my blade on the hill or the glade
  Is music to the corn.
And the old heart of the hill,
It pulses with the thrill,
  And sends its sap aflow;
And it flows into the corn,
And a gladder life is born
  When it hears the song of the hoe.

Hear ye the song of the hoe.
  And what is the song I sing?
'Tis a sweeter rune if your ear is a-tune
  Than the harper's song to the king;
'Tis a song of joy, not of tears,
    How the earth for a million years
  Will bud and blossom and grow,
And still be glad and young
Whenever my song is sung,
  When it hears the song of the hoe.

Hear ye the song of the hoe.
  I sing of the things I hear;
The thoughts down deep in the old earth's
      keep,
  Are whispered in my ear.
And the corn can understand,
And it tells the smiling land
  (Far doth the message go),
The thoughts that have their birth
From the old young heart of the earth,
  That are sung in the song of the hoe.

Hear ye the song of the hoe.
  'Tis an honest song and true,
And good for men again and again,
  And good for you and you.
It sings of the deep-down things,
Of the world's first lore it sings,
  The world-heart's overflow;
And it tells your sallow brood
The heart of the world is good —
  Then hear ye the song of the hoe.

Hear ye the song of the hoe
  That floats with the smell of the soil,
That tells of the wealth of the old earth's
      health,
  Of the metre and music of toil.

And this is the core of its song,
That the earth is made for the strong,
  Nor yields up its wealth to the slow;
And that labor is love and delight
To those who are fain for the fight —
  Then hear ye the song of the hoe.

TOM PHELAN'S HAUNTED BARN

SEE that ol' barn jest over there that's so tipped-up
   an' canted,
That kinder tumble-down affair? — Wall, that ol'
   barn is han'ted.
That used to be Tom Phelan's barn, who died in
   eighty-seven,
Who tried his best for sixty years to fit himself for
   heaven.

Tom said all kinds er piety was nothin' but pre-
   tences
Onless yer mortified yer pride an' kep' down yer
   expenses;
The way, he said, to git to heaven was not by livin'
   gayly —
But you mus' clothe yer back in rags an' scrimp yer
   stomach daily.

He said that he could dress himself three year for
   twenty dollars,
By jest renouncin' stockin's, shoes, an' under
   clo'es an' collars,

An' wearin' meal-bag pantaloons — for they wore
jest like iron —
Were jest as good as any dood's, an' easier to try
on.

So in one corner of his barn he rigged a place to
stay there,
An' in col' winter nights he slep' all covered up
with hay there;
An' if his feet got very col' a-sleepin' on his mow
there,
W'y he'd crawl out a little while an' warm 'em on
his cow there.

He had an ol' tin-b'iler stove he uster cook his
meal on,
An' one pertater twice a day (he et it with the peel
on);
He had an apple once a week, an' once when very
sinful
He baked a pan of Johnnycake an' et a half a
tinful.

An' jest to save his candle-light he went to bed at
seven —
An' one night he awoke surprized an' found himself
in heaven.

'He'd changed his barn an' his ol' cow, tied to her
    rattlin' stanchion,
For a gran' home in Paradise an' a celestial man-
    sion.

But up there in his robes of white, amid celestial
    toons there,
He mourned his bedtick overcoat an' meal-bag
    pantaloons there;
The furnishings were far too rich, the draperies too
    extensive;
All the upholstery an' sich he thought was too
    expensive.

An' all the time he walked the streets he skurce
    could keep from ravin'
About the great extravagance of all that golden
    pavin'.
The jasper an' the topaz walls he thought too great
    expense there —
'Twould serve the purpose jest as well — a good
    barbed-wire fence there.

One day he went to Gabriel in very great consarn
    there,
To try to get permission for to build a wooden barn
    there;

When Gabriel refused p'int-blank, his angry soul
 did steer ag'in
Back to this tumble-down ol' barn an' went to livin'
 here ag'in.

An' here at midnight ev'ry night, the ghost of ol'
 Tom Phelan
Gits out its ol' tin-b'iler stove to cook its ghostly
 meal on;
An' people say who hear his sighs an' awful sobs
 an' moanin':
"For Gabriel's extravagance Tom Phelan's ghost is
 groanin'."

AN ART CRITIC

HE's smart, our boarder's smart, they say,
    Say he's almighty smart.
An' what's he do? Wall, what d'ye think?
    A lecturer on art!
A lecturer on art! Good Lord!
    An' what the deuce is art?
A mess of good-for-nothin' gush —
    But our girls think he's smart.
"What's art?" I says to him one day,
    " 'Taint bread, nor cheese, nor meat;
'Taint pie, nor pudd'n', nor corn'-beef,
    Nor nothin' fit to eat."
An' he caved in an' owned right up
    'Twarn't nothin' fit to eat.

My girls take everything he says
    Without a gasp or gulp,
'Bout skulpin' marble images,
    An' fools who love to skulp.
I want no skulpin's in my house,
    No images for me.

"You can't eat images," I says,
  "Then what is their idee?"
"They express the ideel sense," says he.
  "But they aint corn, nor wheat,
Nor flapjacks, succotash, nor pork,
  Nor nothin' fit to eat."
I squelched him, an' he owned right up
  That they warn't fit to eat.

He showed a picture t'other day
  That made a monstrous hit,
A picture of a durned ol' cow
  They said was exquisite.
"How much milk does your picture give?"
  Says I to him one day;
An' you'd ought to seen him wiggle,
  For he didn' know what to say.
"My cows give milk an' make good steak
  That's mighty hard to beat;
But that ar painted cow of yourn,
  Is she good steak to eat?"
He hemmed an' hawed an' squirmed, and
    owned
  That she warn't fit to eat.

Git out with art! Stone images
  An' picture filagree!

O vittles! vittles is the stuff
   That suits the likes of me.
Humph! art or vittles? What's your choice?
   Stone images or pie?
Pictures of cows or cows themselves? —
   "The cows themselves!" say I.
"Yes, Turner's pictures," said the fool,
   "Are very hard to beat."
"Are they best baked or biled?" said I,
   "An' are they fit to eat?"
An' then the fool he owned right up
   That they warn't fit to eat.

THE SONG OF DEWEY'S GUNS

WHAT is this thunder-music from the other side of
    the world,
That pulses through the severing seas and round
    the planet runs?
'Tis the death-song of old Spain floating from the
    Asian main;
There's a tale of crumbling empire in the song of
    Dewey's guns!

The hand that held the sceptre once of all the great
    world seas,
And paved its march with dead men's bones 'neath
    all the circling suns,
Grew faint with deadly fear when that thunder song
    drew near,
For the dirge of Spain was sounded by the song of
    Dewey's guns!

There is music in a cannon yet for all the Sons of
    Peace —
Yea, the porthole's belching anthem is soft music
    to her sons

'When the iron thunder-song sings the death of
    ancient wrong —
And a dying wrong was chanted by the song of
    Dewey's guns.

THE INFIDEL

————

Who is the infidel? 'Tis he
Who deems man's thought should not be free,
Who'd veil truth's faintest ray of light
From breaking on the human sight;
'Tis he who purposes to bind
The slightest fetter on the mind,
Who fears lest wreck and wrong be wrought
To leave man loose with his own thought;
Who, in the clash of brain with brain,
Is fearful lest the truth be slain,
That wrong may win and right may flee —
This is the infidel. 'Tis he.

Who is the infidel? 'Tis he
Who puts a bound on what may be;
Who fears time's upward slope shall end
On some far summit — and descend;
Who trembles lest the long-borne light,
Far-seen, shall lose itself in night;
Who doubts that life shall rise from death
When the old order perisheth;
That all God's spaces may be cross't
And not a single soul be lost —

Who doubts all this, who'er he be,
This is the infidel.   'Tis he.

Who is the infidel?   'Tis he
Who from his soul's own light would flee;
Who drowns with creeds of noise and din
The still small voice that speaks within;
'Tis he whose jangled soul has leaned
To that bad lesson of the fiend,
That worlds roll on in lawless dance,
Nowhither through the gulfs of chance;
And that some feet may never press
A pathway through the wilderness
From midnight to the morn-to-be —
This is the infidel.   'Tis he.

Who is the infidel?   'Tis he
Who sees no beauty in a tree;
For whom no world-deep music hides
In the wide anthem of the tides;
For whom no glad bird-carol thrills
From off the million-throated hills;
Who sees no order in the high
Procession of the star-sown sky;
Who never feels his heart beguiled
By the glad prattle of a child;
Who has no dreams of things to be —
This is the infidel.   'Tis he.

LISTEN TO YOURSELF

———

Ah, teacher, let me hear you teach ;
  You have brave words from olden seers,
The lore of those long-bearded men
  Of all the far-off years ;
The gray old thoughts of gray old men
  Beneath the Asian stars,
Brought safe by fate through clashing years
  Of unremembered wars.
And you have read the huddled tomes
  Of many an alcoved shelf ;
But have you stood beneath the stars
  And listened to yourself ?

Ah, teacher, let me hear you teach ;
  You at old sages' feet have sat ;
Know you the man within your coat,
  The man beneath your hat ?
You know the thoughts that shaped the world,
  From far-off centuries blown ;
What says the man who talks with thee
  When thou art all alone ?

Why should I listen to a man
  Who listens at the alcoved shelf?
Man, let me hear a living man
  Who listens to himself.

THE CLASSICS

LET me always read the classics.
  There are bardlings of a day,
Fames from twilight unto twilight;
  But the classics ever stay.
And the classics are the voices
  Of the mountain and the glen
And the multitudinous ocean
  And the city filled with men, —
Voices of a deeper meaning
  Than all drippings of the pen.

Yes, the mountains are a classic,
  And an older word they speak
Than the classics of the Hebrew
  Or the Hindoo or the Greek.
Dumb are they, like all the classics,
  Till the chosen one draws near,
Who can catch their inner voices
  With the ear behind the ear;
And their words are high and mystic, —
  But the chosen one can hear.

And the ocean is a classic.
　Where's the scribe shall read its word,
Word grown old before the Attic
　Or Ionian bards were heard,
Word once whispered unto Homer,
　Sown within his fruitful heart, —
And he caught a broken message,
　But he only heard a part.
Listen, thou; forget the babblings
　And the pedantries of art.

And the city is a classic, —
　Aye, the city filled with men;
Here the comic, epic, tragic,
　Beyond painting of the pen.
And who rightly reads the classic
　Of the city, million-trod,
Ranges farther than the sky-line,
　Burrows deeper than the sod,
And his soul beholds the secrets
　Of the mysteries of God.

Give to me to read these classics: —
　Life is short from youth to age;
But its fleetness is not wasted
　If I master but a page.

THE TWINS

I

Two babes were born.   The fields of corn,
Laved in the lushness of the morn,
And murmurous stretches of tall grain,
Waved round the birthplace of the twain.
And sentinel hills around the glen
Kept guard about the twin-born men, —
  Twin-born beside a country lane,
  Their sundered lots and lives made plain
  The twinless nature of the twain.

Above the gleams of mountain streams
For one there loomed the Wraith of Dreams,
And ever motioned with her hand
To some far height in some far land,
To some far land of high emprise
Where unknown seas meet unknown skies. —
  And forth he fared and travelled far
  To lands beneath the Morning Star,
  And where the Sunset Islands are.

"Oh, far away doth Beauty stray
Beside the distant founts of day."

He followed till these founts were found,
And saw her footprint on the ground,
Where she had leaped to take her flight
On to the distant baths of night.
　　But at the baths of night afar
　　Her robe, that sparkles like the spar,
　　Vanished behind a lonely star.

Through shadows gray he groped his way,
Through dim old lands of yesterday,
And where, lapped in a shipless sea,
The empires of to-morrow be.
And far o'er misty mounts and meads
He chased the Vision that Recedes.
　　He chased through morning's rosy light
　　And through the falling mists of night
　　The white Wraith of the Backward Flight.

Borne far along from hills of song
He heard dim, murmurous anthems throng;
When through the desert he had come
He found the Hills of Song were dumb;
But from their skyey summits he
Saw through far mist the Halcyon Sea.
　　When near the sea he heard the roar
　　Of angry breakers evermore —
　　And shattered wrecks were on the shore.

O'er sea and sand through every land
This Pilgrim of the Reaching Hand,
This Traveller of the Forward Gaze,
Fared for a weary length of days.
His Phantom beckoned and was gone,
The Phantom-chaser followed on. —
   His grave is in a lonely land,
   By rainless skies forever scanned,
   And vultures scream above the sand.

II

The twin-born child lived in his wild
And native mountains reconciled,
And there within his valley curled
Fed on the largess of the world;
And there, among his lowly peers,
He drank the fulness of the years.
   With Nature's thought the hills were thrilled,
   Her thought was through the skies distilled —
   His soul was open, and was filled.

The brook that flees through lowland leas
Knows all the secrets of the seas;
And from the brook beside his door
He gathered every ocean's lore.
And there were galleons of cloud
From seas no ship had ever ploughed,

Aerial merchantmen that swim
From Fancy's farthest islands dim,
To bring their freight of dreams to him.

And there were trees where every breeze
Played its Eolian melodies;
And Orient voices in the wind,
Sang of the morning of mankind;
And every morn the unsullied dew
Proved the world's morning still was new.
    The orchard songster's hymn of praise
    Showed him how near were Eden's lays,
    How far away the evil days.

Through forests lone and overblown
Of night winds came a deeper tone;
There did the wind's loud anthems roll
Cathedral thoughts that fill the soul,
Great themes, from no vain babblings spun,
That weave man's thought and God's as one.
    He heard these anthems in the air
    That brought him thoughts he might not
        share,
    Far thoughts — for every thought was prayer.

So resting here without a fear,
The Vision that Recedes drew near.

Each day approached with friendlier grace
The smiling calmness of her face;
Each day he saw with new surprise
The nearing beauty of her eyes.
   He sleeps beneath a mossy mound
   That strawberry-tendrils twine around,
   And apple-blossoms strew the ground.

THE WARMING OF THE HANDS

—————

I warmed both hands before the fire of life.
WALTER SAVAGE LANDOR.

" 'Tis cold," the idle cynic cries,
    " The winds are bleak, the way is bare,
No warmth is in the wintry skies,
    The drifts are everywhere;
And we are stung with shafts of sleet,
    And smitten by the breath of frost;
On life's cold beaches tempest-beat
    The curdled seas are tossed."
Ah, good man, leave the icy sands,
    The wintry shore and sea at strife;
Stretch forth your palms, and warm both hands
    Before the fire of life.

Good man, 'tis not the wintry skies,
    'Tis not the frozen mountains old;
Within, within, your torpor lies,
    Your heart within is cold.
Dulled by the blighting fogs that roll
    Around the lowland fens of doubt,

Upon the hearthstone of your soul
  The fires have all gone out.
Let once again the blackened brands
  Feel the warm flames' aspiring strife —
Stretch forth your arms, and warm both hands
  Before the fire of life.

Upon the hearthstone of the soul
  Still let the genial flame burn clear —
Without the surly tempests roll
  And blast the ruined year;
Without the storms roar far and wide,
  The ruffian winds are fierce and strong —
Around the heart's warm ingleside
  Is heard the voice of song.
The warmth within the soul withstands
  The outward winter's angry strife;
Heap up the blaze, and warm both hands
  Before the fire of life.

You cynic of the drifted snow,
  The blasted fields, the barren sand,
Ah, there are vales where zephyrs blow
  Their fragrance round the land;
Where the deep rose's swelling breast
  Drinks beauty from the summer air,
And where the laughing meads are dressed
  In robes of maiden-hair.

And life is sweet in those glad lands,
　　The air with summer scents is rife;
Go taste its warmth, and warm both hands
　　Before the fire of life.

The snow is in your wintry sense,
　　The ice is in your frozen heart;
Then drive December's torpor hence,
　　And see the mayflowers start.
Behold!　The pageant of the spring
　　Sweeps down the music-haunted glen,
And songs of praise the woodlands sing,
　　And all hearts cry, "Amen."
It is the heart's own ingle brands
　　Make summer peace of winter's strife;
Stretch forth your palms, and warm both hands
　　Before the fire of life.

THE PEDIGREE OF THE DOLLARS

I

TEN good one-dollar bills one day
Within a good man's wallet lay.

And he resolved (so good was he)
To trace each dollar's pedigree;

And not to spend a single bill
That bore a stain of wrong or ill.

So like a sleuth he followed back
Each dollar bill upon its track.

II

Bill Number One he found was made
In a dishonest jockey trade;

And Two a grocer made of late
By overcharge and underweight;

And Three was made through watered milk,
And Four by selling damaged silk;

And Number Five a sweater made
Through starving women underpaid;

And Six was made in dens of shame,
And Seven in a gambling game;

And Number Eight he found to be
The price of wretched perjury;

And Nine was from a robber's clan,
Ten stolen from a murdered man

III

Our good man would not spend again
This money dark with many a stain,

And so he yielded up his breath,
And with his money starved to death.

Ten good one-dollar bills that day
Within that dead man's wallet lay.

They'd never found a man, ah me!
Who'd used them half as ill as he.

ON THE DOOR-KNOB

DEATH's hand is like a brother's hand when stretched
 toward one that's old,
When resting on the white thin locks, the bowed and
 burdened back ;
But to warm youth his heavy hand is very, very
 cold : —
The white crape on the door-knob is darker than the
 black.

Ah, many a tired world-dimmed eye has seen Death's
 face and smiled,
And followed toward his beckoning hand and cared
 not to turn back ;
But why should this stern stranger guest approach
 the little child ? —
The white crape on the door-knob is darker than
 the black.

The black crape on the door-knob makes grave the
 careless eye,
And gives the dullest heart a sense of life's eternal
 lack,

The black crape on the door-knob awes every passer-
 by : —
But the white crape on the door-knob is darker than
 the black.

AN INSPECTOR

For many years I was self-appointed inspector of snow-storms and rain-storms, and did my duty faithfully.

THOREAU.

I'M an inspector on my rounds
    For what I can detect;
Forever, tireless, night and day,
    Inspectors should inspect.
A spy, a spotter keen, am I,
    Whose business 'tis to pry
Into the secrets of the earth,
    The ocean, and the sky.
I'm out on my detective trail,
    And work the whole year through,
And in my business hitherto
    I've learned a thing or two.

Ah, there are mighty goings-on
    Where mighty secrets lurk;
My business 'tis to hide myself,
    And watch the whole thing work.
A few revealments from the sea,
    A few, too, from the sky,

And many secrets from the stars
  And from the winds have I.
And there are whisperings from the fields,
  And tattlings from the mere ;
And 'tis my trick to hide myself,
  Keep still, and overhear.

And, do you know, a little flower
  Has secrets to rehearse,
And tales of wonder from the soul
  Of the great universe ?
And, if you once could understand
  The whisperings of the grass,
And muffled murmurs of the flags
  That grow in the morass,
You'd hear the secret of the soul
  That lives in earth and star,
And learn its inner mystery,
  And know things as they are.

And, could a man go in the woods
  And overhear the trees,
And hide himself within the cliffs
  And listen to the seas,
And could authentically translate
  The language of the brook,
He'd learn some thoughts not hitherto
  Put down in any book.

Could he translate the mountain winds,
   Their voices manifold,
He'd get some thoughts, perchance, too great
   For any book to hold.

   So, an inspector of the winds,
      Detective of the sky,
   Investigator of the brooks
      And hills and woods, am I.
   I have no shame to spy about
      And listen far and near,
   For Nature has no secret thought
      That's bad for me to hear.
   I seek the secret of the soul
      That lives in earth and star,
   To learn its inner mystery,
      And know things as they are.

THE MAN WHO UNDERSTOOD MAN

THERE was a man who understood music,
    And right at the very next door
There was a man who understood science —
    And neither knew anything more.
And next to him was a metaphysician
    Of deep psychological lore,
And next to him was a great theologian —
    And neither knew anything more.
And all around these was a business crew,
Who attended to business — and that's all they
        knew.

And it happened the man who understood music
    Was the dreariest kind of bore —
A bore to the man who understood science,
    Who lived at the very next door.
And they both were bores to the metaphysician,
    And both were incurably dreary;
And all of the three made the great theologian
    Most unintermittently weary.
And the men all around them, the business crew,
With none of the four had the first thing to do.

For the musical man told the scientist man
   All the musical lore that he knew;
And the scientist man did the musical man
   With his scientist volleys pursue.
And every day did the great theologian
   The metaphysician assail,
That he might disembogue in his palpitant ear
   His long metaphysical tale.
For every one reached for the other one's ear —
All wanted to talk and none wanted to hear.

And often it happened the metaphysician
   To the business people would rant
Of Spencer, Spinoza, Heraclitus, Plato,
   Protagoras, Schelling, and Kant.
And the business men, while the metaphysician
   Through his logical labyrinth glides,
Are thinking of dry goods and leather and lumber
   And hardware and horses and hides.
Each overstretched intellect uttered his word —
And every one lectured and nobody heard.

But there was a man who understood man, sir,
   And he never knew anything more.
They all poured their wisdom in showers upon
    him —
   He begged they'd continue to pour.

" Oh, tell me of music, and tell me of science,
    And deep metaphysical lore."
And he'd sit and he'd listen in wondering silence,
    And hungrily ask them for more.
And they made him the leader of all their clan —
This wise ignoramus who understood man.

This wise ignoramus who understood man, sir,
    Seemed raptured, astounded, and dazed ;
At the width and the wealth of their wise erudition
    He'd sit in deep wonder amazed !
And he gulped all the flood of their deep-flowing
        knowledge
    In hungry voracity down ;
So he came to the town where these other men lived,
    And became the first man of the town.
And they thought him the deepest of all their clan —
This wise ignoramus who understood man.

A THOUGHT

———

THE world was bleak and empty and cold,
And wretched and hopeless and very old ;
God gave me a Thought — a new world grew —
The Thought re-created the world anew.

1898 AND 1562

THE evening and the morning have joined in fight
    at last.
  Around the Western islands the Old shall fight the
    New;
Columbia and Hispania, the Present and the Past,
  And Eighteen Hundred and Ninety-eight fights
    Fifteen Sixty-two.

The Nation of the Forward Look that sees the
    heights ahead
  Fights with the Backward Glancing Realm that
    sees the tombs behind.
And who shall doubt the conflict of the Quick and
    of the Dead,
  Of the Leaders with the Laggards of Mankind?

To-day joins fight with Yesterday; the mediæval
    years
  Are grappling with the Modern, and the Old as-
    sails the New.

But who, who fears the issue ? Where's the trem-
    bling soul that fears
When Eighteen Hundred and Ninety-eight fights
    Fifteen Sixty-two ?

A CONTRAST

THE prairies flaunt with grain on every hand;
   The cornfields' emerald banners proudly flare
   Like flags of triumph on the summer air;
The orchards in their fruited fulness stand;
Each breeze with harvest promises is bland;
   The lushness of a million meadows fair
   Exhales its odorous blessing everywhere,
And careless plenty lolls through all the land.

But strong men starve, and dying infants draw
   From breasts of dying mothers, whose wan looks,
     Pain-disciplined, meet death's without a fear,—
To hunger's eye death loses all his awe.
   And here, ye deep-browed writers of long books,
     Look ye! there's stuff for many a folio here.

THE BLOSSOMING OF IGDRASIL

WHY ended not the world when Shakespeare died?
  When the old World-Tree's topmost bloom uprears
  And shows the perfect flower that hath no peers,
Slow fate's consummate bloom and darling pride,
Why longer should its flowerless trunk abide?
  Why lengthen out, sport of the high gods' jeers,
  The anti-climax of its after years
In bloomless barrenness unjustified?

Ah, me, the World-Tree's root strikes very deep
  Down to the midmost core of central strength,
    And draws its life-sap through long winding
      ways:
New life some day shall through its branches creep,
  And on its topmost bough shall bloom at length
    Another Shakespeare — after many days.

THE VOICES OF THE TIDES

"I HEAR the Voices when the tide comes in,"
    Said the old sailor standing on the shore.
    On this bleak coast, above this wintry roar,
I hear the winds of summer and the din
Of bird-songs in the palm-trees.   I have been
    Among the Isles of Beauty; and once more
    The summer seas on Eden headlands pour —
I hear the Voices when the tide comes in.

The tide of time flows in upon the world,
    And breaks on Northern headlands white with
      snow,
    And some there be who hear discordant din;
But close I listen where its waves are hurled,
    And I hear music from far islands blow —
    I hear the Voices when the tides come in.

www.ingramcontent.com/pod-product-compliance
Lightning Source LLC
Chambersburg PA
CBHW021125020726
47500CB00003B/929